Acknowledgment

Most books are the result of the creative forces of more than the writer. Dear Bonnie is no exception. So I'd like to try to thank some of my dear ones who have made this book possible.

My children Eileen and Robert Cohn have been the source of encouragement when confidence lagged. Heartfelt and deepest gratitude to them and to my grandson Jacob Speaks whose never-ending kindness, generosity of spirit plus the gift of so much of his time have made this book a reality. Jacob's literary background and expertise give this effort any quality it may have. Special thanks to photographer and friend Bob Mayeri for his generous contribution.

Of course, without the sometimes perplexing and always devoted Bonnie who brings to life memories of my dear departed but lifelong friend Blanche Rogoff, there would be no correspondence. Perhaps Bonnie will insinuate herself further into the consciousness of the writer and the reader again before too long.

Table of Contents

1. Introduction — 1
2. Oh for Those Good Ole Days — 3
3. Time-Out for Summertime — 10
4. My Friend the Chair — 13
5. From an Accidental Historian — 26
6. The Conch Shell — 29
7. Did You Hear Something? — 34
8. A Season Dying — 37
9. A Case of Double Vision — 40
10. That Other Me — 42
11. Just Wondering — 45
12. A Consequence — 47
13. Is Fall a Season? — 53
14. A Matter of the Times — 55
15. Past Tense — 59

Dear Bonnie

Letters to a Friend

by

Anne E. Cohn

Copyright © 2014 by Anne E. Cohn

All rights reserved.

No portion of this work my be reproduced or stored on any storage devise without the express written consent of the copyright holder. Brief exceptions may be made for passages to be used for review purposes.

ISBN 978-0-87121-091-3

For more information please contact:
alec2612@gmail.com

16. The Revelation	62
17. Ode to Our Temple	65
18. Newsbreak	69
19. And Another Thing	73
20. An Unrequested Report	76
21. More Questions Than Answers	79
22. The Samovar	82
23. A Gift from the Heart	86
24. The Way We Are	89
25. Don't Look at Me!	93
26. A Notable Return	99
27. More Than a Portrait	103
28. About Grandmothers	106
29. Just Between Us	112
30. Coming Home	117

1. Introduction

Dear Bonnie,

   Your most welcome letter arrived in this afternoon's mail and I loved it. I can't seem to get accustomed to not having you around and available for sharing our lives these past few years. Of course there's nothing like an old and trusted friend. I know you agree.

   We've had so many great times together in the past. Even now that both our histories are becoming quite long, it's lovely to have someone who really knows how it all happened and who understands but who doesn't judge. We're probably like a lot of other parents who have cut their roots and moved to be near their children. Thank heavens the U.S. Postal Service has come to the rescue. There really isn't anything quite like a letter for expressing the true attitude and warmth of the writer and also the pleasure and gratification of the reader. (I realize the opposite could also be true but that doesn't apply in our case. So let's not start a whole debate about this).

   Most people may think that an interesting social life is over for us seniors. You can tell them differently. As for me, I must admit things are slowing down. You asked about Frank.

Well, I must tell you that I'm on the verge of breaking off that friendship. It's bringing me more vexation than pleasure. One evening recently he and I arrived a full hour late for dinner with a nice group because of his complete disregard for time. The hostess took one look at me, even though I hadn't said a word, and told me, "Don't ever play poker". Remember you once said I would make a good candidate for the Strasberg School of Method Acting because of that same weakness. Some things never change.

Have you given any more consideration to going down to Florida with me next winter? I'm hoping you will decide to say "yes". Write soon. I'll be waiting for news of what's going on now and also your future plans.

My best love to you and all the family,

                Amelia

2. Oh for Those Good Ole Days

Dear Bonnie,

    I was thinking of sending you an e-mail. However, after contending with all the electric signals in my life, decided to just get out my old yellow Mikado pencil and write.

    Excuse me a minute, the front doorbell just signaled it needs attention. That was my neighbor checking out her exercise timer. Now answering my door involves, not only a bell but chimes as well – a new addition from my security system. Oh dear, I hope all is well with you these days. By any chance, are a lot of things ringing and buzzing at your house too?

    My days usually start with a beep from my microwave oven and go on from there with telephones ringing and various bells and buzzers that continually startle my well-being as the sun progresses and even into the night. Right now my electric toothbrush is blinking, but I'm not sure if that means it needs charging or is over-charged. Thank goodness it can't make any violent noises.

Spring has been really beautiful in Alabama this year and now flowers and growing things are beginning to come into full bloom. In fact, my tomato plants are actually bearing fruit. Yesterday I noticed the leaves were curling and looking a bit wilted----needing some water. Well, I left the hose dripping near them and went on about my business. Later that night, while almost dropping off to sleep, I remembered the hose and got up from bed to turn off the water.

Feeling very efficient, I opened the back door, went out onto my little patio and turned off the spigot. In a few seconds the security alarm went off. (I'd completely forgotten turning it on before going to bed earlier). Before I could get back in the house to turn it off, bells started ringing and a formidable and ugly blast filled the air. The police would probably be at my door any minute. Trying to avert that possibility, I turned off the alarm and quickly got out the ADQ Security handbook and telephoned the police number listed.

They hadn't yet been alerted and suggested that I call the ADQ Security Center. When I finally got them on the line, they seemed to be a bit suspicious and demanded my password. My password?? I didn't remember anything at all about a password but decided to plunge ahead with my bank password. Thank heavens it worked. All immediately became calm again on the home front. About this time the phone rang. It was Richard checking to see if all was well after having been put on alert by the security people. He didn't require a password and was happy to be able to go back to sleep. Seems the more he and Ellen try to make my life easier – the more disquiet I produce for everybody. Do you have a security system at your house? I find mine most "alarming".

Bonnie, are you planning to do any traveling this summer? If so, think about spending some time with me here in Alabama. We could have a good time in spite of all my modern conveniences. Maybe we can enjoy a few quiet days at the Boathouse. It's so peaceful and uncomplicated out there on the river. Water always has such a pleasant and calming influence. And there isn't even a TV on the premises.

You remember Beth, my oldest friend from childhood? Yesterday we spent the afternoon together, then went out to a nice dinner and had an all-round lovely time. After dropping her off, I continued on home at a leisurely pace. There's not much traffic to worry about on Sunday night. Even though there are a lot of buttons on my car that I'm not familiar with, if they don't bother me, I just don't bother them. So it really was a nice quiet ride.

On reaching my street and nearly home, I noticed a vehicle with flashing lights following me. Who that was and why they were blinking all those lights, I had no idea. About a block from my house a siren sounded. Looking in my rear view mirror again, I noticed the car had "Police" painted on the side of the door. Oh gosh!

It was a police car. I pulled over to the side of the road, wondering but not feeling guilty or concerned. A policeman got out and came over to my car and asked for my driver's license.

"Lady," he said, "Don't you know that when a police car flashes its lights, you should stop and pull over?"

"Well, Officer," I replied, "I did notice lights flashing but couldn't imagine it had anything to do with me."

"You made a right turn on a red light back there in the village," he continued.

"I know," I answered, "I thought it was OK. There wasn't any traffic coming either way."

With great patience, he addressed me again. "That was a five road intersection. Right turns on red are not permitted there. Didn't you see the sign? That was dangerous. You couldn't see down all those streets." (I could see down all streets but thought it best not to press the point.)

The officer hadn't taken out his book or pen so I figured this was just going to be a warning. However, I did tell him about my recent test at the UAB Driving Clinic. He didn't seem to be at all impressed.

"I guess your course didn't cover this infraction," he told me, and he continued to lecture me about safe driving for some time. Of course, I felt like an idiot - an old idiot.

Then, on a friendly note, I informed him," I live just across the street."

He answered, "I know, at Carriage Place. I looked you up by your car license".

Since he seemed to know all about me, I thought it only polite to ask him for his name. It's Sergeant Echols. What a nice young man! I was lucky there. Maybe I reminded him of his grandmother.

On opening the door back at my house, I hurried to turn off the alarm before there was a repeat of my last unfortunate experience with that mysterious addition to my life. Ah, the blissful silence! Not exactly so! This time it was the answering machine beeping to announce a message from a friend.

It's very nice to be remembered. Still I just can't face the thought of pushing any more buttons today. Tomorrow will have to do for more high tech usage.

Really, Bonnie, I may not be able to go back into my kitchen for a while. It's filled with buttons and buzzers and things that go beep and hum and ring. Right now I feel like I'd rather starve than confront those denizens any time soon.

Please write and tell me when to expect you. Make it an old fashioned letter – preferably written in pencil on notebook paper. Hearing from you is always a treat. Happily my postman doesn't even carry a whistle.

Give my love to all the family and a special love to you,

    Amelia

3. Time Out for Summertime

Dear Bonnie,

    I'm so glad to learn you are having such a nice visit with Hazel's family up in the North Country. It must be beautiful up there in the mountains, cool and relaxing away from the city.

    Do you remember when there were natural springs and small wooden hotels nestling in the hills near most small Alabama towns? There wasn't much to do in those enclaves of gentle society. People were just enjoying the cool nights and peaceful atmosphere while they waited for summer's heat to diminish and give way to lovely fall weather.

    In our houses too, the pace of life slowed down in the face of hot summer days. Carpets were rolled up off the floors and cotton slipcovers installed on heavily upholstered furniture. Front porches once again came into prominence. Rocking chairs out there, usually neglected, now wore sparkling white cotton covers and were used regularly as a comfortable place to greet neighbors and to watch the children play on the cool grass lawns at dusk.

Now we rush from our air-conditioned cars to our air-conditioned homes, keep up our busy schedules and never even notice our neighbors exist.

As a child, did you and your playmates ever run around barefoot in summer and follow the Ice Truck? Our Ice man was generous with the chips of ice left over as he skillfully cut fifty pound squares from the huge blocks of ice he kept away from the sun under a tarpaulin on his truck bed. How we admired his strength as he lifted such weight with huge calipers to deliver his ware to the ice boxes on our back porches.

Whoa!!!! Nostalgia has its place, but this may be getting to be ridiculous. I'll have to admit that my memory might even be a bit selective,

Of course no one would really like to return to those pre air-conditioning days. In truth I may be resenting the way things are now. Every day we are being bombarded with the fearful conditions and unrest in the whole world. There doesn't seem to be much time for peace of mind and ease of spirit. Oh well, a lot of that "good ole days" stuff is probably equally ridiculous.

There's already a nice cool breeze trying to insinuate itself into the air around here today. Summer will soon be just another memory.

It's' about time to start planning activities for the fall and stop dwelling on the past. Do you have anything exciting coming up for the new season? We really are lucky to have so many chances for new beginnings.

How wonderful to have an understanding friend in you to unload on once in a while. Maybe you'd like to "return my serve" soon.

As always I look forward to your letters. My best to all your dear ones and special love to you,

                                        Amelia

4. My Friend the Chair

Dear Bonnie,

   I do appreciate so much you're taking the time to write last week when you are still recovering from your surgery and getting ready to move back here. You are probably forced to make some choices on what possessions to keep and what to leave behind. After all, many of these so called silent companions have shared much of your life. No doubt each one brings back memories from long ago. And surely these moments aren't to be brushed aside as worth nothing.

   Have you ever wondered, as I do, what some particular old and cherished piece would say to you if it had the power of speech? It has been just sitting there observing you and your household for a very long time and really knows about some of your most intimate secrets. Actually something similar has happened to me. I felt that my favorite and oldest chair really did speak to me. You probably remember that beloved chair that has graced our house since some time in 1942. One quiet evening it spoke to me and vividly recounted the past with surprising knowledge and detail.

 My dear and longtime companion, sit down and listen carefully to my version of our affair of the heart and mind.

 You were married at any early age and thought nothing of moving in with your husband's mother and brother in a nearby city. You were so happy to be with your beloved husband and were more than willing to accept all the conditions that accompanied your new life. As the youngest child in your own family with siblings more or less older than you, you were accustomed to finding your own place comfortably among others. Still, over the years you never felt that this was really your home as the "lady of the house" or expressed your taste and personality. You're probably surprised that a mere chair knows all this about you. Well, I'm a very good listener. Besides, humans aren't that difficult to understand.

 When, after about two years, your beautiful, young mother-in-law remarried and moved to another state, your *duties and responsibilities changed. However, you still felt the same about all the household furnishings that were left behind. Those days you moved the furniture around so many times that your dear husband wasn't ever sure where to put his hat when he got home from work. Your favorite reading material was in Better Homes and Gardens, arbiter of decoration and style. And you loved walking to town and browsing through the local stores looking at the lovely home furnishings, sometimes coveting and always dreaming and admiring. The owners didn't seem to mind someone looking over their wares as though the store was a museum.*

I guess it was inevitable that one day you would discover and fall in love with me. I really was very handsome even though only a chair. My high and rounded back was encased in beautiful mahogany and my legs well shaped in the Chippendale style with ball and claw feet. Upholstered in a lovely blue matlasee. I stood majestically waiting for you to take me home. That night you told your husband about your discovery. He promised to go down to the store to see me. Well he was working hard and long hours and this wasn't his top priority. So a number of days passed before he took the time to pick up his young wife and go down to the furniture store to see this "remarkable" chair. You were thrilled to be shopping with your husband for your first important purchase together. What a happy day! He was going to love your find. However, fate had other plans. When you got to the store you were told that chair had already been sold to someone else. Disappointment brought a well of tears to your eyes. Right then I knew we were destined to a special relationship.

Later, I learned your fine young husband secured me from the other buyers and had me delivered to your house and you! How he managed this, he never told you and I don't know either to this day. You were ecstatic and we've all enjoyed each other ever since. You especially loved and appreciated your kind and noble husband more than ever.

I'm sure you had no idea that I knew all this. That incident was only the beginning. . Yes, on your part you've treated me very well and taken good care of me. Sitting in my place of honor, I have witnessed the daily life of all your family I've stood immovably, unable to act, through your joys and sorrows. But I do know it all and could easily write the story of your life and that includes your family as well.

Your first and comfortable house remained our home for over ten years. Rent was frozen at Pre-World War II rates. Your husband was not ready to buy a home because he didn't want to have a mortgage. (This attitude was probably the result of seeing his mother lose her very beautiful home after his father died and the Great Depression ruled over most of the world.) So 944 Chestnut Street became the birth place of your three children and the scene of a happy and busy family life. Our household became a bit more complicated then and sometimes I was hard put to keep up with everything going on. Jerome was your first child and a handsome and bright baby and little boy he became. He was well known around the neighborhood so that for the first time your identity became set and you were known as Jerome's mother. As he grew he filled the promise of his childhood and youth.

Your lovely little girl Lena was named after two powerful women, one very strong and the other very sweet and kind. Lena was still an infant the day WWII was declared over and peace came back to the world. Soon after that your husband sold the family business and opened the first Melvin's. His brother, still in the army in India approved the move and joined the business on his return to the States and to his and our home as before. During the war years, the family business had been declared a defense industry and was doing necessary work. For the first time the army forte nearby brought many young couples with whom you and your husband made lifelong friends. All those strange people sometimes got to be a bit much for me. Still, I could see how happy you were and contained my impulses to tip over when one of those "Yankees" put his feet on me. Luckily all the members of your families in the armed forces survived. From where I sit, except for the horrible news about the Holocaust and the cruelty of Germany and Japan; it looked like life was going to be very sweet and upbeat now.

    Of course there were still trying times ahead. Little Richard developed Celiac disease at about 6 or seven months of age. Celiac was not known at that time and the cure remained almost impossible. Looking for a diagnosis was a difficult task involving trips to a fine pediatric *specialist in Birmingham, Boston and then finally to New York with your starving little son. There Dr. Sidney Valentine Haas, who had discovered The Banana Diet Cure, finally put you on the right track. All of us at home were very worried about our little boy and our house became much too quiet. After two stays in an apartment hotel near his office on the west side of New York, the doctor dismissed his little patient but with many instructions for diet. And it all worked. He became a lovable and normal lad with a mind of his own, I noticed. I actually enjoyed it when he climbed up on me and put his feet on my clean cushion.*

As things calmed down for your family, you and your husband went back to your usual activities inside and outside the home. You had been talking about building your own home. You had even purchased a lot in the best part of town but weren't in a position to build the kind of house you had planned there. So you settled for a bungalow in the eastern part of town.

The ten years in our new home were a time of growth for all the family. I was given a very nice and comfortable place in the bright living room. The front door opened onto this room so I could easily note the comings and goings of everyone. Jerome and Lena walked to school since there was no traffic on the street that led to a path through the grounds of the local Trade School to their grammar school. When Richard reached the right age he followed the same route. I watched them leave all the time and shared in the pleasant goodbyes. Also, the screened porch, which was shielded from the hot summer sun by a large oak tree, was the location for playing card and board games with siblings and friends. How I enjoyed hearing the laughter and even the heated arguments at times. The large back yard was usually filled with neighborhood boys playing basketball and other games. Lena's nice playhouse fitted well there too. I couldn't see what was going on there. But I did hear one of the neighbors (an older widow) ask you one day, "Don't your children ever go someplace else to play?" It was a nice southern way of meaning – "All these kids around here every day are getting on my nerves". But they were growing up, making new friends and developing. Jerome was Bar Mitzvah and what a grand party we had right in our living room and dining room. I really enjoyed that week end. You took a picture of him wearing his Eagle

Scout badge as he stood beside me too. And how I loved seeing Lena and how lovely she was dressed in a new suit and then a ruffled gown when she was chosen sponsor of the football team at school. I also viewed the card games and dinners you hosted for you friends too. And I was rather lonely on the week-ends when the whole family took your small boat and went to nearby lakes for a day of fishing.

However, there were times of sadness too. We were all devastated at the loss of your sister Sonia at age 43. Papa left us about two years later and Mama moved to Gadsden to be near you and your sister Paula. Life was beginning to take many different courses. Jerome was becoming a young man, testing his new freedom and trying to find out what it is all about. And Lena was making new friends, singing and studying piano and dancing like many of the young girls her age. Richard was a normal little boy now and well. His personality, already interesting and appealing, was becoming strong. You had no idea I had perceived all this. Did you? Remember I was right there in the living room. I was right there too when you decided to build your dream house on your lot in the Country Club area.

What an exciting time for us all. So many discussions and decisions. The style was Contemporary Modern if it had a name. There was no doubt about the fact that it was a house built for comfort, entertaining and just plain good living. This time, I didn't fit in the large living room with its vaulted ceiling, large brick fireplace, glass wall of windows and open look. But that didn't matter to me because I took my place in the study with the sofa and the other things I had already spent so much time with and enjoyed. And you all were often with me there. I was still part of the family. Again I was reupholstered and not neglected. That home was your residence for the longest time of your marriage. From there Jerome went off to college and later married, bringing us another Lena. Later, three little grandsons came into our family. (I do consider myself part of the family by this time.) Lena matured, went away to college too and was married right in this house. You can imagine how I felt witnessing all these plans and changes and not being able to put in my two cents. Even so, it all went well and from that union we all got the pleasure of two more grandsons who spent a lot of time at our house. All this time Richard was growing up too even though his path didn't run quite as smoothly. He dropped out of College and became a Hippy and traveling about as he wished, even to Europe at whim. He too finally came back to us and settled down and married a fine young woman. In time that marriage brought us a granddaughter and another grandson. Of course there were losses along the way but celebrations too as one would expect from you both and your close and warm families

Still, on the whole it was a good life and you were getting ready to celebrate your 47th anniversary. Your dear husband wanted to celebrate that one even though you had hosted a big party on your 45th. Maybe he had some kind of premonition. I agreed with the conversations that took place in the study when you both decided to combine that with a family reunion which would include both sides and all your relatives. You were doing a lot of preparation when you got the heart rending news of Melvin's illness. I don't know how you did it but you went on with the original plans for a reunion at Guntersville Lake Lodge. He attended and enjoyed it all. I, of course, got that news second hand but still enjoyed hearing about it. The illness was unforgiving and plodded on as predicted. I did share your tremendous loss, your *devastation and that of all who loved him very deeply. You certainly spent more time in the study now, and when you rested on me how, I wished that I could wrap myself around you and comfort you. Created to be silent as usual, my fate was to be only an observer. Until Now!!!!!*

It was three years later when you decided to sell your dream house and move back to your girlhood home town. I was pleased to be chosen to go with you and also to be placed in your new living room. Here I am a part of your life still, watching you face old age, never giving up on life. I know it hasn't been easy to lose your two older children. I've heard you admit it was like an amputation without anesthetic except the wound never heals. I believe you've been fortunate in the support of family and old and new friends. Most of them have met with my approval----In case you're interested.

I am still strong too. Even at my age and with my new upholstery I don't think that I look my age either. We've been through so many changes together. I could tell you more but you already know just about everything I do, so I hope we'll go on accepting and supporting one another in the same affectionate way for as long as fate allows.

Bonnie, you've probably had about all you can take of this letter. You already knew most of what my chair remembers. I just thought you might ponder about how our surroundings influence us and vice versa. Try not to work too hard and remember not to discard too many of your belongings of many years. Sometimes these old and familiar old friends can be a source of real comfort.

Best love to all,

Amelia

5. From an Accidental Historian

Dear Bonnie,

I'm so glad you had such nice company and that you feel happily rejuvenated by all the energy and high spirits of the younger members of your family. I know they came from far and wide, even from Israel and China. What a beautiful expression of love and devotion. Is a trip to Florida still a possibility?

This will probably be my last letter dated this year. What a speedy twelve months! They just flew by. I know this is a trite observation but golly it's so true even though I can't remember much if anything about last January. Can you?

On the other hand, everything that has happened since July 24th is imprinted on my brain. That's when my life, as I knew it, "went to pot". Maybe my body just decided to rebel. Have you ever had a similar experience? After all your birthday trails mine by less than a year.

Please excuse my obsessive and complete self-absorption today. I write you because I decided these thoughts that have been chasing about my brain probably should be faced and voiced and you're the lucky recipient. Hope you won't mind.

Have you ever had this experience? You speak of some event or idea that was common knowledge in the past to find that your younger companion has no notion at all as to what you're talking about. Never heard of it. One day recently the name Barrymore came up in conversation. Well, my young companion assumed we were talking about Drew Barrymore. She had apparently never heard of John, Lionel or Ethel (but then I'll have to admit I don't know of their predecessors in that great acting family). What I resent is that these young people seem to think that people like me are a curious repository of quaint and unimportant information with no relevance to the present. Maybe looking back at the past has no compensation unless one is a historian. Sometimes I really do feel like some kind of "accidental historian" at that.

It seems to me that the present is changing almost too fast to keep up with even though we may be better informed than any past generation. But are we better informed and are we that different from people in the past?

From all the above you've probably surmised that I haven't exactly been overwhelmed by a busy social life. I am feeling much improved and stronger every day and more like my normal self. However, there's no exciting news from this end. Maybe you have something of that kind to send me. Really Bonnie, I'd be very interested in knowing what you've found out about life in general.

From the window near my desk I see a lovely valley filled with blossoming fruit trees. Today that gorgeous view is tinged with a bit of fear. Remember last years devastating late frost? My dear, does past experience preclude unadulterated joy for us? What do you think?

Write soon. If you don't feel like diving into the above, just ignore it and send me some jokes.

Special love to you and all yours,

Amelia

6. The Conch Shell

Dear Bonnie,

   I'm so sorry our plans for a return to Florida together didn't work out this year. We had such pleasant times there in the past. Still, you would probably like to know something about my trip "sans" you.

   I did go down to Florida as I wrote you. It was a hard decision to make it on my own without you as a companion. But I haven't given up on harassing you into coming. And I hope you are giving this vacation some thought. Maybe you will change your mind when I tell you how the visit is going for me.

   It was almost dark when I arrived at La Maison du Soleil on Fiesta Keys last Saturday. There was a cool breeze in the air at our favorite of the West-Florida beaches and I must admit I felt a cold chill go through me as well. The front desk was closed so I found my keys in the usual place. Even the bright apartment we remember was proving a bit of a disappointment – the rooms looked so much smaller than before, "Oh well", I told myself.

"You're just tired. Everything will be better in the morning." And so it was.

Opening the drapes in the living room the next morning, I was greeted by a bright and sunny day. The white sandy beach and blue gulf waters were even more beautiful than expected. There was not a cloud in the special clear, sunny sky. I had my breakfast on the balcony bathed in happiness. The present was beginning to take precedence over fond memories of the past winters on Fiesta Key.

Going out to the beach later, I stopped to lock my door. As I turned around, one of my neighbors greeted me. "Welcome to La Maison. My name is Mabel. Would you like to join a group of us on the roof garden for cocktails this afternoon? We usually meet at sunset". Of course I accepted readily and right then began to feel less lonesome and more like smiling. Everyone I met in the halls was pleasant and friendly and greeted me warmly. Actually these people seemed less insular than those in the past. It had taken a while to be accepted then.

Walking past the tennis courts, I noticed all the players were really young. In those other days, men of retirement age, many with white hair, were on the courts, playing hard, trying to keep up their athletic skills – not always successfully. My friend Lou had been a formidable opponent. Now he was just fair. Still he was having a great time.

I put on my sun hat and continued on to the swimming pool. There was not one single person swimming or sun bathing that I recognized here, where in the past we met and made plans for the day and evening. I remember getting out of the warm water and rushing to the sauna and laughing with friends. We had such a good time. Most of us took advantage of the great performances at the Van Wetzel, the opera season, the Bridge Nights and of course dining out together. We usually paired up for the Thursday Tea Dances at Michaels on those mornings too. How we loved to dance! But that was all many years ago.

This is today, the present. What about meeting on the roof garden for cocktails? At dusk I made my way up there and was greeted by tinkling glasses and talk and laughter. Mabel met me at the door and introduced me to the others. They were definitely enjoying each other. Still, they were ready to receive a new-comer. "Where are you from?" one asked. She was from the South too, Virginia. "Isn't that setting sun a marvel?" And it was. The red and gold colors in the sky were gathering together to make a gigantic ball of fire soon to disappear beyond the horizon.

   Deep in light conversation with new acquaintances, I was suddenly brought up short by a sound I had never heard before. It was primitive for sure and suggestive of some far off Pacific island. To my surprise the sound was being produced by Mabel. She had her mouth on a conch shell and was blowing it vigorously. People had gathered on the beach below us and were clapping and cheering. Apparently the Conch Shell Ritual was well known here. Mabel explained it to me. The conch shell is blown to welcome some special event or happening, spreading the news. Here and now the glorious sunset was a magnificent work of nature to remember and cherish. Everyone must be told and given the chance to share in its beauty and wonder.

   I felt my spirits rise within me and the seed of an understanding begin. Could it be that life's sunset is its most beautiful time also? Are the colors and shades of experience gathering together within us to make each person a special phenomenon something like the sun set? Of course, we don't compare with the importance of the sun. But in our own little way and in our own little world we may emulate that concept.

I was lighter on my feet as I rose to leave the party. It wasn't just the pleasant climate and gentling ambience of the place. It was the people here who were bent on enjoying the great and the small. "See you all tomorrow – same time, same place, and same celebration of every day. Hope Mabel brings the conch shell. I know she will".

My first day back at La Maison du Soleil has been much more fulfilling than I ever imagined. Maybe you'll decide to join me here before the season ends. I know it would be good for you. Consider this invitation as the sound of a conch shell portending a great event and beckoning you to return to Fiesta Key.

My best to you and all your loved ones always,

Amelia

7. Did You Hear Something?

Dear Bonnie,

The time here at La Maison is passing pleasantly and much too quickly. New friends have added some zest. Even so, I thought I'd try to look up some of the group from a few years back. No luck so far - until yesterday.

On the beach for my morning walk, dressed in my floppy, sun-proof outfit and wearing an indescribable old straw hat, I was going along at my usual pace when I began to feel that someone was staring at me. When I looked around, sure enough a couple seemed to be looking in a peculiar way and whispering to each other. Apparently they were trying to decide if they knew me and whether or not to speak. Well I continued on to the big rock that marked the turn-around point for walkers. There, I felt a light tap on my shoulder. It was the lady of the couple.

"My husband thinks he remembers you from a few years back. Did you spend the winter on Fiesta Key about eight or ten years ago? And did you stay at La Maison?" she asked.

"Yes". I answered as I removed my disreputable sun hat. You look familiar too. Did I know you then?"

With that, the gentleman, still erect and with a full head of white hair, smiled and asked, "Do you remember going fishing with me?"

I looked at him and immediately remembered the nice younger man who had just retired as Aide to a very famous U.S. Admiral. And indeed he had taken me fishing from the dock of a friend on Short Ship Key and then to a nearby park on the bay.

Offering my hand I replied, "I certainly do remember you Bernie and your kindness and that happy time. Your hair was a dark brown then, I believe".

He laughed and presented his wife. "I guess you don't remember Gladys. She was allergic to the sun in those days and didn't get out much before dark"

"I do remember you, Gladys" I said. "We even exchanged New Year cards for a few years, didn't we?"

My memory was returning. Gladys had been Head Mistress at a prestigious all-girls school in the Washington area. They are staying on Fiesta Key for a while this winter and suggested we get together for dinner soon.

As they were leaving, Bernie leaned over and whispered, "There's someone I'd like you to meet. He's an excellent fisherman."

"By the way", I shouted as we parted, "Did we catch anything that day?"

Well, it looks like any day can bring a nice surprise. I don't remember hearing the conch shell at sunset yesterday. Mabel has been away for the past week so I wonder about that. Guess I just didn't notice.

Write soon and let me know what's going on in your part of the world.

Kisses to all the family and special love to you,

Amelia

8. A Season Dying

Dear Bonnie,

    Your letter was most welcome and I'm glad to hear you are feeling well enough to get out for some social life. How did you enjoy the symphony concert? Do you like the new conductor? I hear he has unbelievable credentials and has conducted world renowned orchestras. Things here are quiet and relaxing. In fact, I'm getting a little tired of all this peace and quiet.

    Remember I wrote you about seeing an old acquaintance who offered to have a friend call me? Well, he did. On the phone his melodious voice was strong and masculine. So I agreed to meet him at the Coffee Shop across the street yesterday afternoon. Prompt as usual, I arrived a little early and was seated at a table facing the large front window. Soon I spied a man who looked like he belonged to the right age group - not bad looking. On further inspection, I noticed he walked on his toes completely destroying the image his voice had evoked over the telephone. Oh well, we had coffee and started to get acquainted. I liked his kind manner with the waitress.

The conversation never did get around to fishing. But I did learn that his favorite singer is Elvis. He did ask me to have dinner with him the next night. He arrived at my apartment on time and had made reservations at one of the better restaurants. All in all he was a perfect gentleman, very attentive. I must admit I was beginning to feel kind of special in his care. We even found we knew some of the same people

There isn't much else to report on this meeting. The next day he was leaving for his home up North and I soon will be doing the same to mine in the Deep South. Neither of us seemed to feel any desire to continue or nurture our new friendship at the present time. I doubt if anything of interest will develop here. Still, what can one expect at our age? I suppose the eternal optimist in me will always see a better future ahead someplace though I must say I don't see it involving anybody.

Since the season here at Fiesta Key is nearly over and spring and Passover will soon be upon us, people are leaving for home and family. On the highway north, they're like a mass of Lemmings bent on their destination.

Soon I'll be joining the throng. Will let you know when to write to my home address.

    Give my special regards to Sam and all the family. Keep in touch.

                                               Love,

                                               Amelia

9. A Case of Double Vision

Dear Bonnie,

Sorry I haven't written sooner. What with coming back home from Fiesta Key and having a bout of some kind of unusual fatigue, the time just got away. I hope you're well and letting the world know you're around and kicking.

A strange thing has happened to me lately. I seem to have a constant companion. It's an old lady (says she's 94 years old and I believe her) who seems to be wherever I am. She knows everything about my past and all my loved ones from the beginning of memory. At times she does leave. For example: when I'm putting on my makeup and dressing to go out, her pale face disappears altogether.

Of course, I look around and there she is again and she tires very easily. You know that kind of thing is rather contagious so I soon feel my strength ebbing too. She loves company and the arts and wants to go to the theater. So far all that hasn't worked out for either of us. She even insists on being at my exercise and physical therapy lately. Her circle of friends has grown smaller with time and so has mine. We even have a few of the same maladies.

I am planning to get away from this worrisome phenomenon. Next week I have some luncheon dates and meetings (including book club) in the offing. I'll let you know how it all turns out.

Today I picked up the phone to call my grandson and family who are with the diplomatic corps in Turkey. They answered quickly as if they were next door, these modern times are really quite wonderful when you think about it. And I think nothing of speaking to kith and kin all over the U.S. just about every day. I suppose we really are lucky to have these advantages.

Enough about me. What great plans do you have in the offering? Are you spending the holiday season at home this year? My constant companion (whom I told you about) is making me think twice about making travel plans. Maybe you can come to see me before long. Let me know.

Give my best regards to all your family and keep special love to you,

Amelia

10. That Other Me

Dear Bonnie,

I loved hearing from you, especially the part about your new friend. How nice that you're going with someone who enjoys the same things you do. (Maybe that's why people flock to performances at arenas, large and small, everywhere.)   In my last letter I told you about my constant companion. That old lady I recently identified as "that other me". She has become so verbal and strong lately that I've found it necessary to give her a name: "Amelia Sr." We have our differences of opinion on a number of matters and sometimes end up arguing. For one thing, she insists on constantly reminding me of my age and not in a complimentary way. I'll just give you one example.

Recently we (Amelia Sr. and I) have become friendly with a lovely young woman who appears to enjoy our company. She generously gives us the gift of her time and presence often. I think she really does want to get to know us and people of our generation. Amelia Sr. feels a bit differently. The other day she told me that this young woman was just using me. When I asked how, I was told, "She's using you as a meal ticket ". "Well, if she is, it's worth the expense" I replied and continued, "In fact we are using her too. We're using her to remind us of the sweet joy of just being alive-- of the excitement engendered by the thought of what tomorrow might bring. We are using her most of all to witness again the utter thoughtless feeling of strength from inexperience - the very "audacity of youth!"

Our beautiful young friend has no need to watch her diet because of weight or other physical issues. So tonight I plan to cook the most delicious meal I can think of, using real butter and all that good stuff. On the other hand, maybe we should just eat out as Amelia Sr. advises.

You asked about Frank. I still hear from him occasionally. He phoned the other day, did the expected perfunctory question about how I was feeling and then didn't listen to my answer as usual. He told me he was calling to find out if I could tell him something about F. Scott Fitzgerald. Apparently Frank had never heard of Fitzgerald but had read something about a new museum in Montgomery dedicated to the lives if F. Scott and Zelda.

Like a dummy, I related what I knew about the subject while remembering one of the reasons I had called off seeing him. Later I came to my senses and realized that the question was probably just an excuse for making the call. At this time of life, I must admit it feels good to be remembered by anyone.

Thank goodness I'm feeling well enough to release some of my help and today I have my house to myself (not counting Amelia Sr.). The glory of the peace and quiet of privacy!

Write when you get the chance. I look forward to my trek to the mail box every day even though most of my mail consists of requests for contributions to worthwhile organizations. I now have enough return-address labels to last the lifetime of everybody in town.

My love to all the kiddies and much to yourself. Amelia Sr. sends best too,

Amelia

11. Just Wondering

Dear Bonnie,

You haven't had time to answer my last letter, I know, but I find I must write you today because your reply to another question is necessary. Recently I've read that if a thought is not expressed, it dies. This thought may not be that important to many people. However, for some reason I can't sleep until I get it out. Hope you won't mind my saddling you with it.

Since I've been at home so much lately and not feeling 100%, doing crossword puzzles has proven a good means of relaxing. Seeing one clue for a four letter word has sparked this whole line of thought. That clue is "Jacob's brother" We all know the Bible story about the two brothers. I've wondered from time to time about why those stories have lived through the ages. To me, they haven't been especially spiritually uplifting. Why have they endured and been considered important?

Maybe I've been looking for the wrong meanings. Jacob has become a venerated figure and "father of our people". Countless men and boys have carried that name until this day. In my own family very beloved kin have and do bear that name. Have you ever known anyone named Esau?

After all, Jacob did steal his brother's birthright. That doesn't look very nice to me. Still, Jacob isn't censured. Also we're told that Jacob was pushed and abetted by his mother. Is that supposed to take away his guilt? On the other hand, his brother Esau, like many victims since, is painted as very unattractive and unworthy. That goes for groups as well as individuals.

So what have I concluded here? Maybe these Bible stories aren't meant to be some kind of moral or spiritual lesson. Maybe they are just true pictures of human nature for us to look at and learn from. All I have to say about that is "We sure are slow learners ".

Now you can go back to your packing. Please take a rest and sit down and tell me what you think of all this. I am so glad you'll be here for the Holidays and look forward to sharing them with you.

My best to you and yours now and always,

Amelia

12. A Consequence

Dear Bonnie,

 Your newsy letter arrived yesterday. It's good to know you are still doing volunteer work at your public library and at the American Red Cross. Libraries are certainly staying current these days. The one nearest my house offers programs of interest to every age and persuasion. Your mention of The Red Cross was a real god send. It made me remember a story that I should have given more importance and recorded long ago. I'd like to tell you about it now. Okay?

 One morning I was at the writing desk in my library-study working rather languidly, when my helper came in to announce that the repairman had arrived and ushered him into the room. He introduced himself, took up his tool box and continued over to the casement window in order to repair its ailing mechanism.

 As he began to do his job, I glanced at him. He was not a large man. When he took off his hat, I noticed his intelligent face and a head of thinning white silky hair. His carriage showed much self-possession and that he had most probably in the past held positions of some importance. There was no doubt that he was a member of that "Greatest Generation".

The actual task didn't take long. Mr. Bowden, as he was called, gathered his tools together, picked up his hat and spoke to me. "I've heard you are a writer" he said, "and I wonder if you have the time to listen to this story which has occupied my mind for quite a long while."

"Of course", I answered and beckoned him to take a chair nearby. He carefully put down his tool box and hat and after a minute or two began to tell me this true story in his own words:

During World War II I wound up in France with the U.S. Army. We were not sent to Paris but to the north eastern country which at that time was an agricultural area. The village our Unit occupied had been hit hard by the Bosch and then unavoidably by us so that it had been more or less abandoned by its inhabitants. Most of the farm houses had been completely demolished, the rest too damaged for use. Still enough of the place remained to show us what a pleasant and fine old village had flourished there before the war.

Our side was advancing cautiously, when on this particular morning we heard a sound coming from the rubble on our right. It might have been a lost cat or kitten. On investigation we found the sound or whimper was not from some lost animal but from a lovely, young French woman, pitiful in appearance and manner. She was painfully thin, except for her middle which suggested that she was with child. Apparently all her loved ones were dead or had fled the enemy.

She looked at us and pleaded for help. "Can you do anything to find my husband?" I could make out with my poor knowledge of her language. Her eyes spoke more eloquently than her mouth. We tried to offer her food. She did drink water and finally took a little of the food we had to offer. What were we to do with our charge? We were expecting our orders to move out at any moment. Every man in our unit felt responsibility and deep concern. It was a bit ironic because on one hand we had our orders to kill - (after all, it was war) and on the other, concern for saving the life of this appealing person. After a while one of our group remembered The Red Cross stationed not far from us and to the west. We agreed that we should take the young lady to them as we knew she would be cared for there. That same day, without hesitation, we wrapped her in somebody's great coat and delivered her to safety. Even so, we were loath to leave that village the next day when orders were received. We never saw her again. After four more months of heavy fighting, peace was declared. Our war was over. Considering the heat of the battles during those desperate days, the losses in our unit were minimal and we were sent back home. Each of us carried with him his own heavy bag filled with memories. Some were unspeakable and erased from the mind with more or less success. Others have haunted us all our days.

However, that isn't the end of my story. In the 1960's my son, who was born sometime after the war, decided to study abroad and his choice of a university was one located in France. There he met and married a beautiful young girl who was studying in Paris but had been born and brought up in another part of the country. She doesn't know much about her parents because sadly her mother died at her birth. Her father was killed in World War II and therefore she had been lovingly and beautifully brought up by her only aunt and uncle. They all lived on the family farm which had been restored and rebuilt after the War.

When I look at my daughter-in-law, look into her eyes-- I feel deeply that I have known her before, long ago. Now fate has brought her to this place in all the world. Right or wrong, true or false, I know she belongs with us. I once heard an old adage that tells us that if a person saves another's life, he is then compelled to always look after that person. I'm more than willing to be part of that effort along with her devoted husband. He dearly loves and cherishes his gentle wife, at times with some wonder.

Mr. Bowden became quiet. He closed his eyes and then visibly brought himself back to our conversation.

Well, Bonnie, I sat in my chair, tearful and unable to speak; for a few minutes. Then I rose to take his hand and thank him sincerely for sharing his intimate and deep emotional experience. After wishing Mr. Bowden well, I asked for permission to repeat his story. He readily agreed to that and added that he just didn't want this wonderful part of life to be forgotten and to use it as I wished.

One never knows the consequence of any little happening - even a broken window mechanism.

I'll write you later when I get over meeting such an exceptional human being and hearing his story,

Take care of yourself and give my love to all the family,

                Amelia

13. Is Fall a Season?

Dear Bonnie,

Your daughter Betty's letter arrived yesterday and you can imagine my shock on learning about your accident. I am so sorry that you are in the hospital and have had to undergo surgery for a broken femur. I do hope you are not suffering a great deal of pain and discomfort now and will have a swift and uneventful recovery.

Two of my local friends have had similar experiences this past month. They are now in Rehab and will soon go back home for recovery. Surely I'll hear that kind of news from you soon. I'll keep in touch as soon as it's convenient, as I really am quite concerned.

Of course your plans for moving back here will have to be postponed until you've recovered. What a disappointment! Still I'm sure it will all work out - just be a little later in the year. I'll get in touch with Betty and find out if there's anything I can do for you at this end. All our friends were looking forward to your return and already counting on you for Mah Jongg. I'm sure that's the least of your worries right now.

My birthday party won't be the same without you, though. When it was in the planning stage, I wanted to know my job and what to do. I was told that my job is to take care of myself - not fall- and stay well until the happy day. Now I'm beginning to believe that's not really such an easy job. To tell you the truth: I'm scared to death to undertake anything out of the ordinary or to climb the stairs to my studio on the second floor if no one is here with me. I know. You're shaking you head and wondering how long that will last.

You're probably not too interested in all this babble right now. I' m just so accustomed to passing everything by you. Feel much better by the time you get this letter. In the meantime, I'll be concentrating on sending you good and happy vibes.

Love to all the family but especially to you,

Amelia

14. A Matter of the Times

Dear Bonnie,

I am so sorry you were not able to make it here for my birthday party and hope you are feeling much better these days. You were missed and so many people asked about you.

The week end of festivities was a great success, bringing loved ones - family and friends from near and far. The dinner on Saturday night and the party (attended by about a hundred family members and old and new friends) were happily enjoyed by all and reflected the light hearted mood created in part by the decorations, and the refreshments but mainly, I think, because everyone was so glad to see one another. Today, a few days into the following week, I've grown rather reflective myself.

Though my birthday occurred only a few days ago and the fresh flowers are still alive and beautiful, it seems to me that I've entered a strange and new age. After all, when one reaches a year closer to the century mark, it gives one pause. Not only does the past become more vivid, but a kind of curiosity about the near future takes over from memory. That's not an easy task when memory is so strong and clear.

    Just think. We've lived most of our lives in the twentieth century. It never occurred to me to give any thought to the twenty-first century. And now fourteen years into the present century, it's already taken for granted. During my lifetime the history of the Jewish people has witnessed much tragedy and suffering - with the Holocaust and World War I, World War II plus the anti-semitism leading up to that time - even in the free U.S.A. On the other hand, what joy we have known with the birth of Israel and what seemed to be a better understanding and acceptance of the Jewish people. Israel's wars of survival to combat almost constant attacks from the Arab world seemed temporary to the optimistic spirit of the Jewish people. Of course the nineteenth century gave our people the Russian pogroms that brought so many of our parents to these shores. How lucky was my generation to reap the blessings of that fate and the courage of those immigrants.

    And now what can we expect of this Twenty First Century of ours? We hardly noticed the change of date.

During the sixth month of this year we were forced to open our eyes. We started to see the rise of open anti-semitism in Europe and around the world. The dangers to the State of Israel from constant attacks, some only verbal, others by rockets and other weapons of destruction could no longer be ignored. And one begins to wonder, very seriously, what the future has to hold for all the powerless little people of the world.

Here in our own beloved land, one notes a certain lack of compassion for others. I've always thought that the high tech society, with its great source of communication readily available all over the world, would bring about a better understanding between people of diverse backgrounds and experience. Now I wonder. Is it just too early to expect real change? Or does the ability to spread hatred and disrespect by these same means overpower the force for good?

I hope my negative views haven't depressed you. It hasn't even helped me to get it all out of my system. All this when I'd promised myself to write something amusing and light hearted! Please forgive me!

Personally I really am grateful for all the fine and caring people in my life and their expressions of love, understanding and even respect (deserved or not). And I'm grateful for all those to whom I can easily return those sentiments. Guess there's something to being a stubborn survivor!

I look forward to hearing from you soon and until then plan on directing my thoughts and memories to only wonderful, happy thoughts. Remind me of some.

Best to all the family and of course to yourself,

Amelia

15. Past Tense

Dear Bonnie,

    I'm glad to learn that your children will be with you for the holidays. It is a great family time. What's going on with Jennie? Will she be with you? So you're planning a trip. I'm glad you feel up to traveling. As for me, that's not on my agenda any time soon. That other me (Amelia Sr.) I wrote you about precludes any thought of that kind.

    In fact I'm writing you at three a.m. because "Amelia Sr." (that other me) won't let me sleep. Not that there isn't plenty going on to keep me awake, but she brings up the darndest things. Last night she reminded me of the time Beth Fisher and I, who were about 6 years old then, spent days watching a cocoon on her back porch. It must have finally hatched and produced a butterfly because I remember we had a funeral and buried the poor thing on the side of her house.

    Amelia Sr. still wouldn't let me sleep even though I was dead tired. She was still remembering. Before all the streets in Birmingham were paved, every day a cowherd passed our house, on the Sixteenth Street side, as he was driving the neighborhood cows to their grazing grounds someplace up on Fountain Heights.

The other me seems to enjoy these visions of the past. Maybe it's some kind of proof that we were really there - existed then. On the other hand, to me these pictures appear as something seen through the wrong end of a telescope. Still I suppose these visions are less disturbing than thinking of past mistakes and regrets.

On a brighter note, my lovely niece Iris visited for a several days last week and we had a fine time. Amelia Sr. disappeared and wasn't missed. We met for meals with special family and even attended a wonderful symphony concert. She is very pleasant company and accepting and fine all around. Next week will bring grandchildren from far and wide for Thanksgiving. I really mean "Thanks giving".

It's too late to try sleeping again this morning so I'll get up, have some breakfast and try to get rid of my constant companion for a while. I must admit: "Amelia Sr." isn't always hard to be with. She's often the engine by which some very dear memories bring back much happiness.

However, I really do wish we could both concentrate on the present instead.

Please write me when you get the chance. I need to know how active and busy you are and what new thoughts and events are in your life - and people. It's important.

Love to you and everyone at your house,

Amelia Jr. (I guess)

16. The Revelation

Dear Bonnie,

I received your nice letter and, as usual, found it insightful and to the point. It's wonderful to have someone who cares about the things I do. Thank you. Let me share another happening that I find many-faceted. It concerns a recent phone call from my grandson David.

By his middle twenties, David had already experienced life on his own in N.Y.C. and China, and he had traveled around Europe. This past summer he was in Africa exploring Tanzania. He even climbed the famous Kilimanjaro. His interests are so varied and unusual. And I'm lucky enough to be on the receiving end of some of his life experiences. He really should be writing about all this himself, and maybe he will someday. Until then may I talk to you a bit?

Last week David called me, and we had a long conversation. I reminded him of a true story he related to me when he was making his way around Europe. He told me then about meeting an elderly couple in a restaurant where he had worked as a waiter. As he served them every night, they became very friendly, so much so that they even invited him to stay with them at their home. I couldn't remember if all this occurred in Holland or Belgium and was wrong on both counts. In fact, it was in Germany. I reminded David of how kind these people had been to him and how fond of him they were, even taking him to the border when he left for the next country. He told me that, yes, the lady cried when they parted. I asked him if he had written to these people, or made any effort to keep in contact.

My young grandson hesitated and then told me that he hadn't ever written them or made any effort to keep in touch with them. He hesitated again. I could feel some kind of deep tension over the wires.

"Grandma," he told me, "These people were very proud of two elegantly-framed photographs in their home showing each of them in Nazi uniform!"

For a moment, a feeling of palpable shock took my breath away. Rarely had David revealed his inner self to me. I was confounded. Was this fine person just repelled by harsh cruelty? Or did he, in his deep inner self, feel his heartstrings pull to the history and soul of his people? Or both?

I do know one thing; I will never again give him, or any of our young family members, a "subtle" push toward my idea of good behavior without knowing all the facts.

Let me know what you think of this new revelation. Thank you for your usual deep understanding. Write soon, and tell me what you're doing these days.

My best to you and your loved ones as always,

Amelia

17. Ode to Our Temple

Dear Bonnie,

The sad news that our Temple in Gadsden, a place of infinite importance to my life and my dear ones for so many years, is closing its doors. A room at Temple Emanu-El in Birmingham has been given to our community for display of our artifacts and other memorabilia. The enclosed tribute is resting in that place.

Ode to Our Temple

It is with a heavy heart that I pick up my pen to say goodbye to our beloved Temple.

From the time I arrived in Gadsden as a twenty-one year old bride until I left a widow forty-nine years later, Temple Beth Israel had been central to my life. My husband, too, and later our children found in our congregation a loving home where we truly belonged and were always welcome. There we celebrated religious holidays, held our bar mitzvahs and confirmations, attended services and were inspired and comforted.

As I look back on those years, I realize how greatly we were assisted in efforts which inevitably helped in our development. Our years of participation in Temple affairs resulted in encouraging creativity as well as leadership qualities that have served us well in other areas too. I, personally, feel sometimes that our Temple has been my university in many ways. The varied programs and activities (even to studying voice and singing in the choir) have enriched my life and the pleasure of life in general.

My children, too, found a second home at our Temple. There they not only received a good Jewish education but through The Temple Youth Group and the North Alabama Temple Youth Groups made good friends and developed social skills that would prove invaluable as they matured.

During my years in Gadsden our congregation was blessed with outstanding and admirable, really fine and good people who greatly influenced my life. They nurtured me as a young woman and later proved to be loyal, close friends.

The accomplishments of our Temple Sisterhood (originally called The Ladies' Aid Society) fill me with awe. Of course they fulfilled the usual Sisterhood duties at the Temple. Other successful projects also come to mind: the annual Rummage Sale, Flower Bulb Sale and Art Auction also our Jewish Festival Tour of Homes and Israeli Festival. All these affairs were enthusiastically supported by our non-Jewish friends as well.

When our Temple was bombed and two of our members shot, these same neighbors showed us great sympathy and compassion. Our ladies, too, were active in resettling and repatriating two refugee families –one from Nazi occupied Austria and later a couple from Russia. Neither elected to make their permanent homes in Gadsden.

After some time both families moved to larger, more cosmopolitan cities. Our small congregation continued to help them attain their wishes.

I know a Temple is just a building. Yet our beautiful and beloved Temple does reflect the loving care of those who lavished their attention on her through the years. It fills me with sadness to think that the present may bring an end to Temple Beth- Israel's glorious history and contribution to our world. It's hard to lose our dear Temple. When we celebrated Beth-Israel's one hundredth anniversary just a few years ago, its members didn't realize that our house of worship would soon become a concert hall-given to our city for that purpose. Memories are all that remain to comfort the bereaved but we also share gratitude for those memories. Temple Beth-Israel will always remain a great lady!

Bonnie, I'm afraid that Temples in small towns all over our country are closing because of lack of membership. Guess it's just changing times. Still there is regret. I know you have some memories of past times spent in Gadsden with me and know how important our Temple was to all who share those memories. It seems these present times are filled with thoughts of our past lives. Mine are. Do you find this true also?

Give my best love to all the family and let me hear from you when you feel like writing. I always look forward to hearing from you.

       Love,

       Amelia

18. Newsbreak

Dear Bonnie,

Thank you for the beautiful flowers. The bouquet was so lovely and bountiful that we decided to divide the flowers into two vases. One was a lovely picture of mixtures of those star lilies, majestic in a sort of art deco square vase. The pink rose buds soon opened in an unusual white vase about six inches tall and four inches wide in spots but rather flat. It was given to us on one of our trips to Israel and never used until now. I'm planning to paint both pictures and will send you a copy when the paintings are done. That may take quite a while the way my strength is behaving now.

Rushing to the emergency room at the hospital was quite a surprise to me when I returned to consciousness in an ambulance on the way there. Care at the hospital was excellent and for some reason all turned out well. Recovery is a bit slower than I expected. Quite a few things now are not as expected so I guess we are always adjusting to something. Enough of that! I refuse to retreat into my small inner world - even though it is often hard to win the battle over long habits and a mind filled with memories.

When you think of it, the telephone is truly a marvelous invention. Especially now. I'm not talking about all those "intimate" calls from some guy with an interesting, manly (sexy) voice who addresses you by your given name but really wants a contribution to a worthy or unworthy cause of some kind. There are many more really wonderful calls telling us that we're thought about. Almost every day calls are coming through to my house from faraway places. Your experience too, I imagine. I guess nothing is really that far away any more. My grandchildren, and grand nephews and nieces are calling and letting me stay a part of their lives, and of course so are the nieces and nephews. It's just heartwarming. Sad to say that group is a little smaller than when they were younger. Friends have proven loyal and loving too. So I'm not really complaining.

I do have some really fabulous news to relate. Our David is getting married in May. He met the girl while he was studying in China. She had been his teacher of Mandarin Chinese while he was over there. A few months ago, he got his degree here in the US and then hurried back to her and apparently popped the question. Richard and Ellen are leaving for the wedding to take place in Kunming (the city of eternal spring) on April 25th. I'm pleased David's parents will be there by his side. His sister Gail might also get to attend. Wish I could travel and go too. We've had some great conversations, and they are so happy. So are we for them. They plan to make their home here in the U.S.A. That may take a while now that immigration rules have become so complicated. Will let you know.

    Spring is really here in Alabama at last. The pear trees are in blossom looking gorgeous against the blue sky and so are the cherry trees and some apples. Today I noticed the azaleas in my little patio are bursting into full flower and the dogwoods in the front are lovely in color and shape. So are the daffodils around my neighborhood. Mountain Brook is really even more beautiful than I remember from last year. I'm sure you'll be very happy to get back here.

    Just when are you planning to come? By the way I've joined a group called "Aging with Grace." It's interesting and fairly thought provoking. You might like the women in the group too. And heaven knows our Mah Jongg foursome is looking forward to having you back. Half the time now someone is under the weather and can't attend. At times we're driven to play with only three people. They tell me that's a sign of an aging group. But I'm sick and tired of hearing about the age thing, ` Aren't you? Still, I'll let you know in my next letter about that other group.

Please give my special love to all the family and save some for yourself. I miss you, so write when you can and I don't mean e-mail - just an old fashioned letter.

    Always,

                      Amelia

19. And Another Thing

Dear Bonnie,

It was lovely hearing from you. Did you ever get your problems with the social security folks settled? Surely verifying your age should be simple enough.

I remember when social security was inaugurated. That brings me to thinking about all the changes that have taken place during my lifetime. Have you ever thought about this? Everyone wants a long life but nobody really wants to get "old". And what is old anyway?

The funny part of it all is that age creeps up on us when we're not looking. It happens in spite of society's worship of youth and even though a person listened to the warnings and the advice of "youth mavens", exercised, dieted, applied beauty potions and tried to keep a current outlook. It's inevitable that one day the mirror will reflect signs that the years have been adding up.

Oh well. But whatever became of venerating the wisdom gleaned just by living? I really get upset when someone talks to me as if I were three years old. Actually, they expect more from a three year old these days (and children really are pretty smart) Admit you're tired and you'll get more assistance than you bargained for and start feeling that maybe you really should have additional regular help. No! Just stay in the game. There's plenty of time for taking a break or bowing out. For heaven's sake, don't tell anyone you left the keys in your car with the motor running or that sometimes you've noticed a little trouble with your balance. They'll think for sure you are losing your "marbles" and there goes your independence.

Of course, people do mean well. I sometimes think that this new phenomenon of longer life needs getting accustomed to. Maybe society just hasn't learned the best way to face it yet. I guess it is a bit overwhelming. What about isolating and herding people together in the many retirement facilities covering our country now? Of course its big business these days, but what would be an alternative?

What about our generation? Have we changed the world in any appreciable way? Lots of wonderful scientific discoveries have been made – even landing on the moon.

Of course, medicine has gone in many different directions with transplants and new drugs. However, are we a kinder, more compassionate, less judgmental people? Less greedy?

I don't know what brought all this on today. Perhaps I've become a realist. Or is it just a touch of self-righteousness? Do you have a prescription for my ailment? I suspect the best remedy might be a dose of some happy, care-free company, light hearted folk to just share some of the joys available. Any suggestions?

Well, good night, dear. It's time for my beauty sleep. Who am I kidding? I'm just dead tired and have to get up early tomorrow for a session with my personal trainer, then to an afternoon of Mah Jongg. You can't say I'm not trying.

Thanks for letting me bend your ear. Stay well and let me hear from you soon. Are you noticing any of the subjects I am finding so perplexing?

Love,

Amelia

20. An Unrequested Report

Dear Bonnie,

Hope all is well with you. Glad the spring thaw has been accompanied by so many nice social affairs and meetings with good friends.

I hope you won't mind but I'd like to relate some of my thoughts about that "Aging with Grace" thing. Why should we have to age with grace? Is it to make those around us more comfortable? And why are we grouped together because of our age? I suppose that's always been the case, though, at other times in our lives. Now everyone seems to be put in a group. First there were the "teenagers" and then the "baby boomers" and more Pre and Post groups. There are a lot of names for us "seniors" too. I don't mind being categorized that way. Still, I find it hard to think of myself as obsolete. Don't you? And I don't have to like it. Maybe that's because it tends to make a person feel shut out of the mainstream of life and that isn't easy for many of us.

I do realize that loss of some physical strength does limit one's activities and maybe loss of a bit of mental capacity goes along with it all. However, I'm wondering if the new way of looking at material things has something to do with it all. Now we don't keep anything that doesn't work as well as it should, nor do we get it fixed. We just throw it away and get new "things". Thank goodness that hasn't taken over the human condition yet. But is there some influence? Thinking we're not important and just tolerated - even though well treated could be the modern way. Sounds like science fiction, doesn't it?

Instead of striving to "age with grace" maybe we should do what William Blake tells us to do about death:

> *Do not go gentle into that good night,*
>
> *Old age should burn and rave at close of day;*
>
> *Rage, rage against the dying of the light.*

Maybe I'm turning into a cynic. That's more than true when it comes to politics and anti-semitism. Gotta stop reading so much and find out how to play more. Gosh that may be the answer to everything! Let's plan to do something outlandish and soon.

I promise to be more upbeat in my next letter and I'm looking feverishly for something pleasantly wonderful to write about. The fact is that I already have happy news from his family about David's wedding and our new Chinese relatives. Be on the lookout for a letter that is almost dancing with joy.

    Give my best to all the family and love to you always,

Amelia

21. More Questions Than Answers

Dear Bonnie,

Your letter arrived today with the wonderful news that you are recovering even more quickly than expected. So now it won't be as long as I thought before you are back here and it will again be "like old times". I look forward to that time but now I must tell you what a pleasure it is to share thoughts and ideas with someone who shares a lot of the past and who always understands me and even agrees with me most of the time. It' no small thing to feel completely at ease, to know one will not be misunderstood and to feel acceptance of one's thoughts and ideas.

I especially enjoyed your response to my last letter. As always the Jewish world looms heavily in my consciousness and you accept that and feel much the same way .The turn of events and new rise of overt anti-Semitism is enough to make a cynic of anyone. You've been thinking about this too, I know. Remember how in our younger and more productive lives we worked so hard to create understanding among all people? All those programs and affairs we spent our energy on and how we labored to educate our neighbors, trying to help them understand and respect the Jewish people? Was that really all for naught as you've come to believe? On one thing I do agree with you 100%.

We don't have to be on the defensive. We shouldn't worry so much about being accepted and valued.

From now on I will respond as you do. If someone makes an anti-semitic remark in my presence, I'll say, "You don't like Jews? That's <u>your</u> problem. I don't like bigots". How is that working for you? You didn't tell me in your letter.

Well, I've gotten that off my chest. And now, if you can stand to hear more, I'll address another issue. You mentioned how you are coping with our age problems. Like me are you finding it strange when people don't realize that under your new appearance, your white hair (sometimes optimistically blonde) and your slightly sagging face and body contours you are the same person you've always been? Not exactly the same of course. We should be a bit wiser. After all, we have certainly been tempered by our life experiences and the people we've loved and those we've lost and what we've learned along the journey.

I've decided that we have become "people of interest". For some reason we are living an unusually long time. As our younger friends and acquaintances begin to reach a new stage in their lives, they may be feeling a bit vulnerable and out of control. Perhaps that makes them curious about us. They wonder how we've survived and they're probably idealizing our personae's, giving us more courage and joie de vivre than we actually possess. Do you think that we are really the gallant creatures they see in us? This is all very flattering. Still, it makes one ponder. Do you think we should be more honest? Or is that absolutely necessary? Oh well, these days maybe we should relish the lovely attention, continue to hold our backs straight and keep on smiling.

Bonnie, take good care of yourself. Be ready for the next change in your life and look forward to our being together again in body as well as spirit. I am.

Special love to you and all the family,

Amelia

22. The Samovar

Dear Bonnie,

   How busy you must be getting ready to break up your house for your move back here. When I think of all you're going through, it makes me appreciate your letters even more than usual. Like me, you have probably collected so much over the years, each article with a history or at least a story. Hope you will take a rest and share one of my stories now.

   This morning at breakfast I happened to look up and on a high shelf, above all the others, noticed an old Samovar, a pre-electric urn, still rather dignified but looking a bit lonely and forlorn. Our Samovar was not made of copper or brass like some that I have seen made into table lamps but of some unidentifiable Russian metal. There was writing on it but none of us could read Russian to get any kind of information.

   We do know that the Samovar came to us when uncle Label passed away. My dear husband and I were rather close to this uncle and believed he wanted his treasured possession to remain in the family. We were named to carry out his wishes and I felt it my duty to do so even after I became widowed. Uncle Label had made a return trip to his home in Russia some years after immigrating to the U.S. and probably this Samovar had accompanied him back to Alabama.

There is no doubt that our Samovar has presided over many "Teas". Probably most of these were small family affairs, and probably at meal time. As far as we are concerned, there was only one time it was fired up and used. That occasion I remember vividly.

It happened some years ago when my mother and father were still alive. They had come to visit - just for a few days to get away from their usual routine. They had been badly wounded by the sudden cruel loss of my beautiful and lively sister Sarah and I anxiously tried to relieve their sorrow and mine.

I remember vividly my parents having tea when I was a little girl. The tea leaves were packaged in a small tin trunk, painted red with straps in gold so that it looked very real. Like other children of that time, I used the empty trunk, after the tea was all gone, to store my valuables like paper doll clothes and jacks.

Even though I didn't have any of that Swee-Toch-Nee tea, maybe we could bring out the Samovar and make tea as they had long ago when they were still young. Papa knew how to fire it up with the pieces of charcoal I had provided, and we would brew tea the Russian way, adding boiling water from the Samovar. We sat around the small cloth covered table and drank our tea from my best china teacups with mandel bread slices. How delicious it was. I'm not sure any of this brought back memories of the past. Still, It really was a success anyway and very much enjoyed by all. Even the Samovar seemed to have regained its sheen. Perhaps it was feeling useful and part of the family again after long neglect.

I must confess, Bonnie, our Samovar has not been used again since that day. Maybe making a lamp from a Samovar isn't such an insult after all. At least it would be out among people and doing a job. One doesn't have to be a purist. But, No! I'm sure our proud Russian expatriate wouldn't approve.

Please let me know if I can be of any help from this end. At least I did make you stop and rest from your labors for a while to read the above. Write me when you have time.

Best love to you and all the family,

Amelia

23. A Gift from the Heart

Dear Bonnie,

I've been thinking about you today and wondering if you know how much your friendship and many acts of kindness have meant to me over the years. That brought to mind the idea that one doesn't have to be a great hero in order to have a real impact on others. Even small acts of kindness are important and much cherished. You probably already know all about this.

Anyway, did you ever know Sister Rose Frances at our local Catholic hospital? As a nun, of course, she had chosen to give her life in service to others. Sister was small in physical statue, not ethereal but rather matter-of-fact and even feisty at times. In fact, in later years she became the absolute ruler of the hospital parking lot. Woe to anyone who broke the rules in that province.

Sister Rose Frances once told me about her experience on coming to our small southern town to help open a Catholic hospital sometime in the late 1920's or 30's. The Catholic population in Alabama was small and rather suspect. So the hospital was not well received. At first no local people chose to use that facility. Sister was from Brooklyn, N. Y. and only 16 years old at the time. She remembered those days when there were no patients to care for, and every day the sisters would scrub and clean and wait to be needed. Finally a surgeon, who was a company doctor for the local steel mill, brought in a patient for surgery. Little by little the Catholic hospital grew and became a respected and valued local institution.

    I tell you all this just to introduce Sister Rose Frances who by the time I am recounting was getting to be just past middle age. She took a personal interest in her patients and once phoned my dear husband to help her in the care of a Jewish patient (a jewelry salesman from Brooklyn) who had had a heart attack while calling on a local jeweler. But that's another story.

    This time she called Melvin to ask a real personal favor. Her sister was visiting her and Alabama for the first time. Did he know anyone in Birmingham who could show them around? Of course he did and called my brother Iz. You remember him – an out-going and friendly fellow if I do say so. Iz had a friend, who was a Presbyterian minister, join the party. The visiting nuns had a grand tour of Birmingham and were taken to lunch at that private, posh club on the brow of Red Mountain. There they enjoyed a nice meal and a super view of the city spread out below them.

Some months later Melvin had to undergo serious surgery and was recuperating in our local Catholic hospital. Iz came up to visit him one Sunday and Sister Rose Frances found out that he was in the building and hurried to Melvin's room to greet her former host. She asked to be allowed to return as she had something for Iz in appreciation of that wonderful day in Birmingham.

In a short time Sister did reappear - with her Harmonica – and proceeded to give a Harmonica concert!!!   It was truly a gift of the heart from one who had renounced worldly goods.

Bonnie, I'm sorry I can't play the harmonica for you. Still, perhaps you'll accept this little true story of generous spirit instead.

Love,

Amelia

24. The Way We Are

Dear Bonnie,

It was lovely hearing from you as usual. I really do enjoy thinking of your point of view which is sometimes very different from mine. Not too long ago I had occasion to call on a bereaved family member and the experience set me to thinking about human nature. You'll notice that I have taken some liberties in order to get my point across and written this more like a narrative (which it isn't).

The Way We Are

Joseph had been an unusually handsome young man. Now things had changed and he was old and looked it. Even his name had been changed when he landed on Ellis Island from the old country. His life would never be the same now with the death of his wife of more than fifty years.

Even so, some things had always stayed the same. Joseph continued to practice the teachings of his youth and carried out, without fail, the religious practices and traditions of his youth.

Tonight he was covering the mirrors in his home as he sadly received friends and family who were expressing sympathy and sharing his mourning period.

Both of his sons had inherited their father's good looks and were making a success in business, living a life totally foreign to Joseph. Tonight they conversed in a lively manner even though bereaved by the loss of their strong and beloved mother. On this evening they were already looking forward to a golf game together and talking enthusiastically about past games, the "birdies" made, the golf courses they'd played and enjoyed.- conversation strange to the ears of their father and completely incongruous to others present.

After all the guests had left, the sons reverted to their youth, and became boys again. They began to help their father put the house back in order and get ready for bed. Harold, the older son, stayed the night so his father would not be alone.

Now the house was quiet as Harold lay down in his old bed for sleep. However, sleep didn't seem to want to come. Instead a flood of memories took over. He remembered hearing that as a youth in Europe his father had worked with a relative who was a chemist. So there were some skills and knowledge which he planned to put to use in his new home in America. Joseph was pressed to make a living for his family. He had dreams of big business -- bottling vinegar and selling it for domestic use. His knowledge of chemistry spurred this endeavor and Joseph worked hard. He wanted the respect of his American born wife who was proving more dominating as the years passed.

The son remembered too, how his disappointed mother had complained about their poor financial condition, not moving up to a finer house and neighborhood. Little by little his father had become quieter and more withdrawn. His jaunty, youthful walk was disappearing. Was this new world beating him down?

Harold's memory filled with pictures of his gentle father taking him by the hand to school and synagogue. In summer Joseph had shown him and his brother how to swim and play ball. The son could almost feel the wind on his face as he had so long ago when riding with his father to deliver bottles of vinegar.

Harold's heart suddenly filled with love and empathy for his dear father. He got up, went to his father's room, leaned over the bed and kissed old Joseph on his wrinkled cheek.

The next morning was sunny and clear. Someone was making noises in the kitchen, probably preparing breakfast, but that was of no interest to Harold as he got up and started dressing for his golf game. He was looking forward to meeting his brother at the golf club.

"I'll see you later, Papa," the son called as he hurried out the front door.

Bonnie, please let me hear from you and let me know what Jack writes. Does he like his new position? I'm beginning to think a lot of things are generational and have always been. Oh well, no one ever said that life is easy to understand. My best love to all and especially you,

Amelia

25. Don't Look at Me!

Dear Bonnie,

I learned some time ago that nothing stays the same. That truism has hit me again on losing my oldest and dearest friend Beth a few weeks ago. I've outlived almost all of my closest family members and loved ones who made my life. And now Beth has joined them. There's really no one left who actually shares a host of memories of the long ago past. When you think about it, you find that is an irreplaceable and deep loss, making memory a lonely journey. This dear friend became a part of my life when we were still children - long before you and I had the good fortune to meet.

Maybe my heart and head can be eased a bit by telling you about Beth and me. Having always taken her presence for granted, I need to step back and take a good look. Will you go with me?

Beth and I met at Temple Beth-El's Sunday School when we were about ten years old. Both of us have cherished our relationship from childhood to maturity and even into old age. Really old age! We almost always (except in rain) walked down 14th Ave. S. on Sunday mornings to the small white building housing Temple Beth-El then. I lived on 13th Pl. S. and Beth near 15th St. S. So I'd go by her apartment and pick her up. Beth was always petite and pretty with black curly hair and a ready smile. She often wore a yellow wool skirt and matching sweater that I admired and probably coveted.

I was the youngest of four children in my family. My siblings were from six to eleven years my seniors. She had two older brothers and a younger sister. My parents had been immigrants from Russia. Becoming "American" wasn't easy for them as they always had strong attachments to "home". My mother especially missed her family and Russian culture. Papa, out in the world making a living, didn't talk about the past and seemed to adjust better to this new world with some ease. Of course our home life and family values were a strong influence in our view of the future. My sisters were typical older Jewish sisters and doted on me. My brother was growing into a very attractive man. All worked and helped at home.

Beth's parents were American born – had no foreign accents. Her grandmother was still living and sometimes with her family. (I never knew mine personally). Her lovely mother was a wonderful home-maker and cook. Her father, attractive and masculine looking, was a travelling salesman. So I rarely saw him. Her two older, handsome brothers were making their way in the world and society. Her sister was still a little girl.

In spite of the differences in our families, we each felt perfectly at home at the others home. Often we spent the night at one another's house and enjoyed being together. All this took place during our country's deep depression when just about everyone was suffering from financial problems. It was expected then that after High School, we both go to work. I started out at a local Jobbing Co. at $8.00 per week salary. Beth got a job working for a local Insurance agent for $7.00 per week. She was probably worth her pay. I wonder if I was. We met for lunch almost every day, belonged to the same club and shared a lot of the same friends from High School and" Young Judea" days.

At my wedding to Melvin, Beth and Melvin's brother Abram were the only people to cry. They needn't have. We held fast to both of them always. Beth would often come to Gadsden on weekends. We remained close friends after our marriages and while rearing our children, through widowhood and whatever fate held for us. Beth's second marriage brought more grown children into her life. Her generous heart enfolded them and in return they did the same.

When I moved back to Birmingham in 1989, it was like old times. Almost! Sadly, serious illnesses that Beth had suffered in the past were taking a toll on her independence now. She finally gave up her lovely home of so many years and moved into a retirement facility. She had her own apartment, was in what they called independent living and was as friendly and feisty as ever. She still liked to cook and bake and was probably the only occupant who owned a freezer which she kept packed to capacity as usual. With her special companion and driver of almost fifteen years, she was able to continue her life as she desired- attending Temple services, social and community events and the inevitable shopping, beauty shop appointments et al.

At her retirement facility, of course mostly occupied by older people, some changes became evident. People everywhere were using walkers to improve balance and aid in walking. On any day the hall outside the dining room was lined with walkers. Still inside the dining room there was talking and laughing and obvious enjoyment of the food and company. Also, more and more the emergency folks and ambulance drivers showed up. They were picking up the ill and victims of accidents like falling as is their mission.

   Beth and I were visiting more over the phone now. One day she told me this: "I was walking down the hall yesterday when I met up with two of those 911 guys carrying a stretcher. When they reached me, I told them, *don't look at me. I'm just going to the dining room*". Her sense of humor remained intact. However, when a few weeks later she told me she didn't feel like going to the dining room to meet her friends for dinner, I knew something was very wrong.

   Some days after that, the "911 guys" did come for her. As fate would have it, I happened to be with her and was until the end. What a loss for her dear family and myriad of friends. Now I often find myself at the telephone ready to call her- not realizing she won't be able to answer. Still

I must finally come to terms with this loss and know that she has now joined all those other loved ones in memory……..so many.

Thank you for listening and caring.

My best to you always,

                              Amelia

26. A Notable Return

Dear Bonnie,

You asked about my experiences since beginning to do some tutoring at my old elementary school- Glen Iris School. It has really been very meaningful to me.

You might be interested in the following story I wrote for my students. Of course, there is a lot of truth in it. Some might be emotional truth. Anyway, let me know what you think of all this reminiscing.

A Notable Return

An elderly lady drove up to Glen Iris Elementary School, parked her car and walked confidently to the entrance as she remembered it. When she put out her hand to open the door, she stopped short in puzzlement. There wasn't any door to open. In fact, there was no entrance.

This lady had signed up as a volunteer to tutor first graders learning to read. She had enjoyed reading all her life and wanted very much to pass on that pleasure to this generation of students. The first session was supposed to begin in about ten minutes. Besides, Glen Iris was a place she thought of with much affection. As a little girl she had spent her first years of school there a long time ago. "The entrance used to be right here", she thought. "Things are bound to change over the years, I guess".

Looking down the left side of the building, the handsome wall around the patio outside the old lunchroom was still as it was many years ago. The red brick was trimmed with white stone as were other parts of the building. However, there was no entrance visible on that side of the school. The new tutor turned and started down the other side. What happened to the parallel bars and swings of long ago? Where were the girls' and boys' soft ball diamonds? Now the building covered all that ground. Farther down were more buildings and raised beds for flowers and other plants. The school building now covered an entire square block. On reaching the next corner, she looked around to her left and there was the entrance at last – right in the middle of the block. On each side of the covered entrance beautiful flowers and shrubs welcomed visitors and, of course, students and teachers. "So this is Glen Iris Elementary today", thought this lady, "It's very large and impressive".

As she entered the school building, the future tutor was greeted by Dr. Wilson, Glen Iris' principal, who welcomed her warmly and directed her past the library and to Mrs. Jones' first grade class room. That was the beginning of a very happy experience. Our tutor now looked forward to Tuesdays when she would meet with her very nice and appealing students and their teacher. On getting to know Mrs. Jones, it became clear why almost everyone remembers their first grade teacher with love and affection.

Some people might think that Glen Iris is just a large brick building near U.A.B. It is that in a way. People who are lucky enough to enter that building find the building isn't only Glen Iris Elementary. The school has a certain spirit with a warm life of its own and is a very special place – a very important place for many. The students and teachers and staff really make it. The students come from a variety of backgrounds. Some have parents who were born in foreign countries and are speaking their native language at home, just learning English. All this adds a rich flavor to the school experience here. These students and its graduates of different ages, now scattered over the country and world, will always value their time at Glen

Iris. It was and is a wonderful place to start one's education and to begin a useful and meaningful life.

Just ask our tutor about Glen Iris. She has now found the entrance to the present building and cherishes her past and present association with its endearing children who are full of promise and the joy of life. The future certainly looks grand when you look at it from Glen Iris Elementary!

Bonnie, please share some of your experiences with me. Any similar happenings? Write soon and I promise to concentrate on the present in your response. My best to you and all your family as well.

Love always,

Amelia

27. More Than a Portrait

Dear Bonnie,

    I haven't heard from you in response to my last letter. However, yesterday something remarkable happened to me and I just have to share it with someone who will understand it completely and even care.

    Of course you remember Melvin's portrait hanging over the pretty French desk in my living room. Like almost everything else in my house, these items have a special history. The desk was Melvin's gift to me on our second wedding anniversary. The portrait was made in 1985 at the request of Gadsden's Altrusa Club and was to be hung in the City hall to honor Melvin for being awarded recognition for being selected Gadsden's Distinguished Citizen of that year. The picture I have is a copy of the original. A large and well attended ceremony accompanied the award. All this took place right before my dear husband received the shocking sentence that he had less than a year to live. By the time he got around to having the portrait made, that fatal year had already begun to tick away.

Yesterday I stopped to look at Melvin's picture as I often do. This time it pulled me to him and I felt strongly that he was there in person and drawing me to him intimately in the old way we had enjoyed for so many years. His eyes were looking right into mine and his half smile seemed to be telling me that he was still loving and nonjudgmental. I, on the other hand, started to wonder what he was really thinking - thinking of me.

Of course his appearance was showing no signs of the ravages that just living imprints on our faces. Does he notice the changes in me? I know he wouldn't care if he did. Yet I can't help wondering if he would approve of the manner in which I've spent the years so generously allotted to me. He probably wouldn't think I've been a wastrel there. Still what would he think of the company I've kept? At the time I thought he would understand how lonely it was without him.

I wonder if he could know the pain of losing two of our beloved children. Could he ever imagine that such a cataclysm would befall us? If not, I don't think I would be able to tell him and take that smile off his noble face. He so enjoyed our grandchildren whom he knew and loved. I would like to introduce him to the two he didn't get to know and who are such a blessing. Also, I don't think he or I ever had an inkling that we would be great grandparents of four youngsters. It is a miracle to watch their appealing personalities as they grow and mature. Melvin and I are now the root of three generations. Are all these lovely people really our progeny?

I suppose getting to the age when one leads a less active life has the advantages of having the time to calmly, though not without some preformed conclusions, look back on a long life and the people involved. Too much of this sort of thing probably leads to some sort of melancholy.

Today, on the contrary, as I gazed at the portrait again, a beautiful smile actually radiated from Mel's face. He was telling me something - telling me to remember: "Oh, how we danced!"

Bonnie, I know you remember too. Sharing sweet memories with someone who understands and cares is really quite wonderful. Bless you!

Amelia

28. About Grandmothers

Dear Bonnie,

It was wonderful to hear from you and to learn that you are feeling better and will soon be able to continue your plans for moving here. I am looking forward to spending a lot of time with you and making up for the months we have each spent battling the pains that often accompany ill health. That was a "bummer". Wasn't it?

The epidural I was given seems to be working. My legs are back to normal and are functioning without pain. I don't know, and neither do the doctors know, how long this relief from the assault and rebellion of my body will last. During those pre-epidural days the telephone calls and concerns of loved ones made life bearable and really fed my usual optimistic spirit. Like me, you have kin spread to all parts of the world. This morning I was awakened by one of those calls. This one was from my grandson David in China. How lovely!

You remember David was married in May to beautiful Lei Lei. They are living with Lei Lei's grandmother in one of those gigantic apartment houses one sees spread all over "The city of eternal spring" where they reside while working as teachers. You probably remember David who has insatiable curiosity and the courage to act on his quest for knowledge by traveling and living in far off places. He even climbed Kilimanjaro not too long ago. David found his lovely Lei Lei in China so that venture proved to be a huge success. But back to his phone call.

During our conversation David asked me how it felt to be a grandmother. At the time I didn't realize that he was expecting a deeper answer than I could give on the spur of the moment. That question was followed by this story, and I wonder if the story doesn't reveal the importance of his question.

A few days ago Lei Lei's grandmother left her apartment to do some errands which was not an unusual occurrence. However, when she had not returned in several hours, the young couple began to be concerned for her safety. David decided to go down into the neighborhood and look for her. He looked in the markets and small shops near their apartment to no avail and then spread his search out a bit toward the public park. This area was not known to be quiet and peaceful.

Sure enough, David soon came upon a rowdy group of young men fighting. There were already about three or four of them lying on the ground. David looked around and saw a younger man with his hands around the throat of an older person and choking him. Without thinking David approached these two and rescued the older man. Soon he realized the danger of the situation and left the area to continue his search for Grandmother.

In the park he tried to find her and carefully noted everyone he passed on the benches and paths. After a while he noticed a woman sitting on one of the benches and having her back and shoulders massaged. (He didn't tell me the sex of the practitioner). The woman was Lei Lei's grandmother. David approached her and began to reproach her for being out so long and causing them much worry. She didn't apologize. Calmly Grandmother told David to go home and not worry about her. She would return home when she was ready. I don't know how that sounded in Chinese, but David got the message.

I'm wondering now if that experience didn't prompt David's question about how it felt to be a grandmother. Could it be that until now a grandmother filled only one role as he saw it? Maybe he hadn't thought of his grandmothers or Lei Lei's as persons with long histories and lives of interest and devotion to unknown friends and relatives. Also, I'm sure David has been thinking of my age and is curious about how one approaches the last years of one's life.

So what shall I tell him? "How does it feel to be a grandmother?" Gosh, maybe he was about to tell me something about becoming a great grandmother again. There is one thing to be sure of. David will come up with something very interesting and something out of the ordinary. Actually being David's grandmother is very exciting. He gives my life dimensions never expected. To tell the truth, I'm thrilled that he wants to talk to me and gives me some of his time (that precious gift).

The question "How does it feel to be a grandmother?" never occurred to me before now. I do remember thinking it was a kind of miracle when it happened to me as a youngish woman and now, of course, with great grandchildren I sometimes don't know who I am or how it all happened. Being once or twice removed does bring some advantages. I can look on this flesh of my flesh as beloved folk but also as interesting individuals, each with his own personae and gifts.

I never got to know any of my own grandparents except through stories and anecdotes told by my parents. However, I do have very clear memories of my mother-in-law as a grandmother. From that I now realize that one of the blessings of being a grandmother is that one has somehow learned to be completely non-judgmental and to just love and cherish these wonderful children and young people, accept their unconditional love and enjoy them.

I can observe my grown grandchildren with pride and with some wonder. They are all very loving. However, sometimes I'm curious about what they think of me. Do they know anything about me besides my role as grandmother? How can they when I often don't know myself? Of course, we know that this is the way of life and how nature works. Still, I'm afraid it all leaves me with more questions than answers. Please let me know your take on being a grandmother. I'd love to know your thoughts.

Well dear, keep on improving. Can I do anything at this end to see that your new abode will be ready for you?

My best wishes to you and yours for the coming year and always.

    Love,

        Amelia

29. Just Between Us

Dear Bonnie,

I hope you are recovering nicely from your broken femur. I know you haven't felt like writing. I've been thinking of you quite a lot, and most of my thoughts have been related to the idea of making changes in our lives.

Surely you are ready for a change or you wouldn't even be considering giving up your present abode and moving back here, coming back home. So I'm wondering about what you expect on coming back. Am I presuming too much if I feel like warning you that "home" won't be exactly what it used to be? All this might not concern you at all but just be a part of my having too much alone time and becoming too introspective.

Still there's no doubt you'll find "home" different from what you left more than twenty years ago. It might not show up on a visit even if one gets hints of a different kind of place. And twenty odd years of growth and progress in every way has made that true. You may not recognize it as progress when you go downtown, see all the empty buildings and wonder what happened to the usual crowds of people. The department stores we grew up with are no more. They've either moved out to the malls or closed entirely. I can't meet you at the balcony tea room at Loveman's now. Nor can we order our Buffalo Rock float because that large corner is now a children's museum. Of course that is a wonderful facility but you have to admit it's a change even if it is a good thing. The centers of activity have now moved over the mountain to bright new venues offering great coffees and ices and frozen yogurts to name a few. We can meet some fun place any day when you get back. We can also take a ride down town to check on the lofts filling with residents every day and the new businesses resulting from that renaissance.

But don't plan to attend any grand affairs at the old palatial Tutwiler Hotel with its sweeping marble staircase, gorgeous carpets and crystal chandeliers. A hotel with that nostalgic name is now located a few blocks away in a much smaller building. Instead on the corner of 20th street and 5th avenue stands a multi-story office building. Forget about Joy Young's great egg rolls and the lunches we enjoyed there right across the street. That old restaurant moved away and then closed altogether. Now our more cosmopolitan city offers foods from so many other countries and cultures - not just Chinese. We can take a world tour of establishments offering French, Mexican, Thai, Lebanese, Japanese and even Indian cuisine. The Alabama Theatre has been restored but not as just a movie theatre. The Lyric nearby is being slowly restored too. On the other hand we now have a first class concert hall and symphony orchestra and lots of live theatre offering interesting plays. Shall we get season tickets for next year?

You probably remember when the University of Alabama at Birmingham began to grow and their medical center took over the old Jefferson Hospital. Well don't be too amazed when you get back and see how that has grown. Now the school and highly regarded Medical Center is a sprawling complex of new and modern buildings of every description and takes up most of the lower part of what we used to call the "Southside". Both UAB and its medical facility are growing in size and prestige every day and the Medical School is now world renowned.

Be glad you can still drive your car. Those majestic yellow street-cars along with their tracks and electric cables are gone. City buses haven't taken over here either. Our home town has spread out to so many suburbs and small, self-governing communities, it would be hard to figure out routes. Have you decided where you want to live yet? Don't even think about the old neighborhoods. Some are pretty run down and others offer only second rate apartment houses. However, just driving around town, I notice new apartment buildings going up everywhere. Maybe you'd prefer a town-house like mine where you can still enjoy most of your old valued possessions but not have to worry about keeping up the grounds.

    That's just a few of the changes I've noticed. However, the biggest change of all is in the people. When I attend a community affair, the number of strangers present are a bit over powering. These people are newcomers or children and grandchildren of those we knew so well. The Old Guard has perished. Of course you've heard about our intimate friends who have left us during the past few years. We're hard put to keep our Mah Jongg game going even with inviting new acquaintances to join us. That's one place you'll feel hasn't changed much. Or maybe you will see that we too aren't the same. We're definitely showing signs of aging. One of us can't hear very well and another is having a little trouble seeing. Don't worry. We're as feisty as ever = maybe a little crankier at times but you know enough about us to accept us as we are. I find New Horizons at UAB an antidote for all that. It's a stimulating lecture program offering speakers on a variety of subjects and the people who attend are the best part, so interesting and nice to be with. We can attend together if you wish.

So keep on packing and getting ready for the grand welcome awaiting your arrival here and the new and fresh offerings of the future.

My best to all the family and special love to you,

Amelia

30. Coming Home

Dear Bonnie,

I was excited to learn that Marion's husband has been transferred back home. Of course you'll be moving back here soon. How wonderful! I can hardly wait.

You're all invited for dinner on the first night you're available. And you!!! You must come for lunch as soon as possible. It will be like old times getting together for our usual chit chat. While having our tea, we can solve the world's greater problems (and maybe some of our own) even if no one takes heed. Shall I invite Amelia Sr.?

Absolutely not, I think. I really would like to host an "Open House" to re-introduce you and Marian. You are going to be surprised to realize what a cosmopolitan city we've become. "Sure nuff"!

Our Mah Jongg group are thrilled to learn the news of your expected return. In fact, they are all so pepped up by the news that they're looking years younger. They really are. Not only have we missed your company, but we've had a hard time getting the required number of players together on some Wednesdays. Please hold that day open if you can.

Well I suppose we won't be writing letters any longer. Will you miss our correspondence?

My trips to my mail box always filled me with anticipation during these past months. Also, it was rather fulfilling to have to think through thoughts in order to get them down for reading. Perhaps a journal would be a reasonable alternative. I really have enjoyed writing to you and especially receiving your letters. Thank you for being so very kind, receptive and understanding during all these past months.

It is quiet here and calm & lovely- just awaiting your arrival. What a happy feeling!!!

See you soon

Love,

Amelia